CAN YOU IMAGINE?

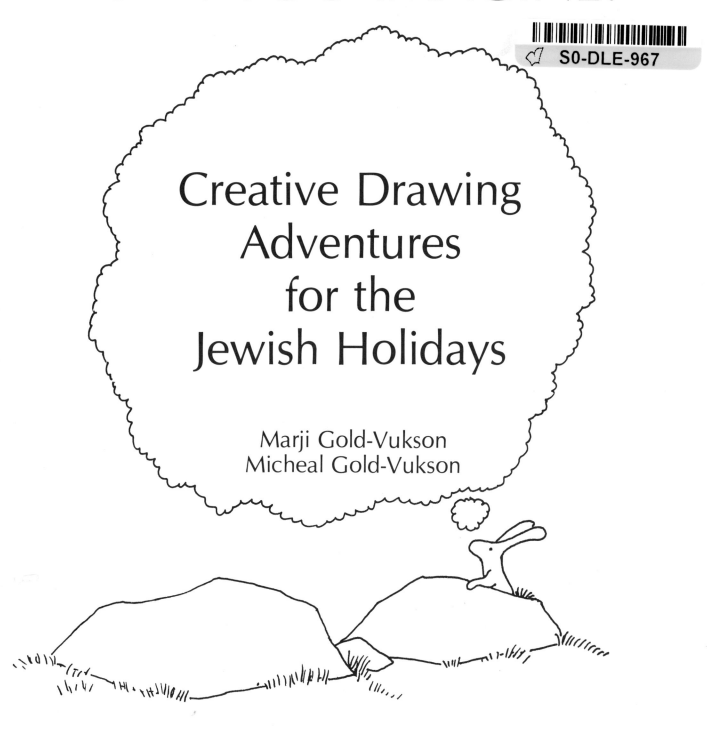

Creative Drawing
Adventures
for the
Jewish Holidays

Marji Gold-Vukson
Micheal Gold-Vukson

KAR-BEN COPIES, INC.   ROCKVILLE, MD

Dear Parents and Teachers,

Welcome to *Can You Imagine*…an exciting new "un-coloring book" for young children. This unique collection of holiday drawing activities has been designed to promote creative thinking, self-expression and artistic exploration.

It's easy to use this book! Simply select a page to coincide with the Jewish holiday you're studying or celebrating, help your child to read the brief instruction, distribute drawing materials, and watch as young imaginations take flight!

Very best wishes,

Marji Gold-Vukson

To Cyrelle Simon, morah extraordinaire.

Library of Congress Cataloging-in-Publication Data

Gold-Vukson, Marji.
   Can you imagine? creative drawing adventures for the Jewish holidays/Marji Gold-Vukson: illustrated by Micheal Gold-Vukson.
       p. cm.
   Summary: Suggests activities involving drawing and the imagination, centered around the Jewish holidays.
   ISBN 0-929371-31-3
   1. Fasts and feasts—Judaism—Juvenile literature. [1. Fasts and feasts—Judaism.]
   I. Gold-Vukson, Micheal, ill. II. Title.
   BM690.G518 1992
   296.4'3—dc20   91-42842
                                                                                          CIP
                                                                                          AC

CONTENTS

We kindle the lights of Sabbath to welcome the day of rest. The aroma of warm challah and sweet wine fills the air. It is a time to visit, to read, and to sing. The Fourth Commandment tells us to remember the Sabbath day to keep it holy. Each week, from sundown Friday until sunset Saturday, we do.

It is autumn. The sounds of the shofar tell us that the New Year is here. On the first day of Tishri we dress in our best clothes and go to the synagogue. We eat apples dipped in honey to get the new year off to a sweet start, and wish each other *l'shanah tovah tikatevu,* may you be inscribed in the Book of Life for a good year!

Soon it's the 10th of Tishri, Yom Kippur, the Day of Atonement. It is a day to fast and to pray, a day to ask forgiveness for our wrongdoings. When the shofar sounds again, Yom Kippur is over. A happy and healthy New Year!

Tishri is a busy month. As Yom Kippur ends, preparations for Sukkot begin. We gaze at the stars through our sukkah's leafy roof, and think of the ancient wanderings of the Jewish people. The graceful lulav and fragrant etrog remind us to be thankful for the yearly harvest.

Rejoice in the Torah! Dance, sing, and wave your flag! On Simchat Torah we read the last section of the Torah…and then begin again by reading the first.

For eight nights, the glow of our Hanukkah menorah warms the wintry night. We eat potato latkes, spin dreidels, exchange gifts, and join in song, to commemorate the victory of the brave Maccabees over the Syrians on the 25th of Kislev more than 2000 years ago.

In Israel, the 15th of Shevat is the beginning of spring and the birthday of the trees. We celebrate by purchasing baby seedlings to be planted in Israel, and by planting seeds ourselves. Try a snack of dates, carob, almonds, and other fruits and nuts that grow in Israel. Oh, and don't forget to hug a tree!

It's the 14th of Adar. We twirl our groggers and stomp our feet as we read how brave Queen Esther saved the Jewish people from wicked Haman's evil plot. With masks on our faces and hamantaschen in our shalach manot baskets, we're ready for the parade.

Passover celebrates our freedom from slavery. In the springtime, on the eve of the 15th of Nisan, we gather at a seder, taste the special foods, and read from the Haggadah about our exodus from Egypt. For eight days we eat matzah to remind us that our ancestors, in their haste to leave Egypt, didn't have time to let their bread rise.

We dance the *hora* and sing *Hatikvah* under a spectacular sky of fireworks. It's the 5th of Iyar. On this day in 1948, Israel's first Prime Minister proclaimed the creation of the new state. Happy Independence Day, Israel!

Between Passover and Shavuot is the period we call the Omer. Lag Ba'Omer is the 33rd day, a day for picnics and outings, a night for bonfires and stories of how Shimon bar Yohai and his students secretly studied Torah in caves, safe from the Roman conquerers.

God gave the Torah to the children of Israel at Mt. Sinai on Shavuot, the 6th of Sivan. Today, we read the Book of Ruth and remember God's blessings and commandments. Our homes and synagogues are filled with fresh flowers and fruit from the spring harvest.

Invent a silly new way to rest on Shabbat. Show how it works.

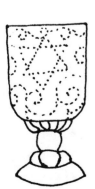

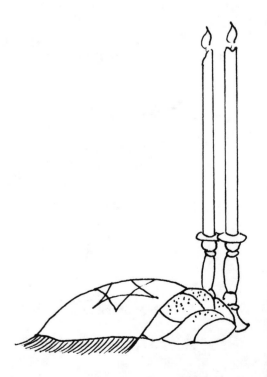

What do you imagine people think about during Shabbat services?

What might you see at a Shabbat celebration on the planet "SABBATHIA"?

Imagine what it would be like to meet the Sabbath Queen.

Suppose you dipped an apple into a bowl of honey… and something *very* surprising happened! Draw what happened.

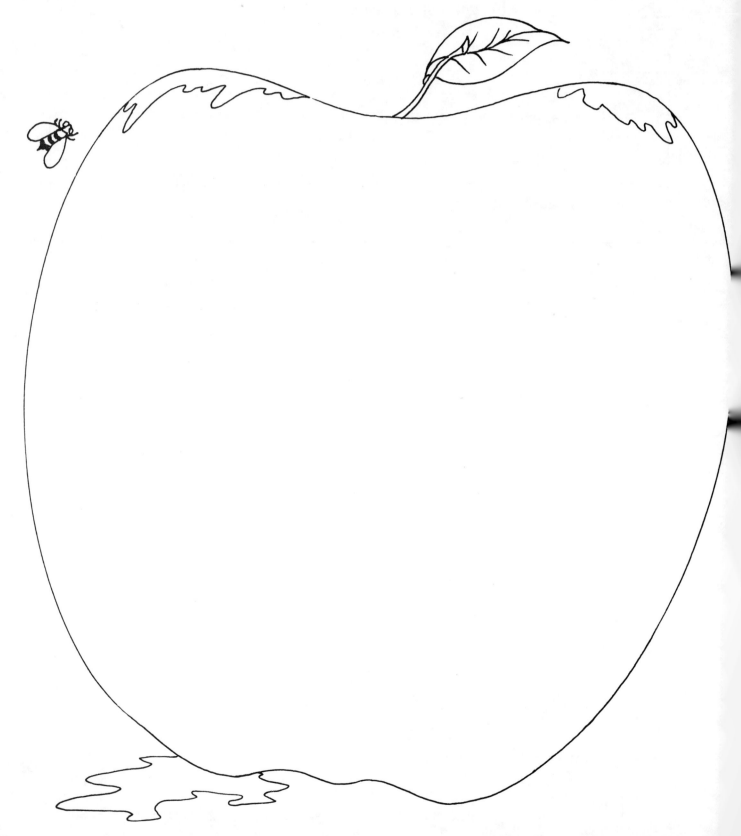

Decorate this special cake for Rosh Hashanah, the "Birthday of the World."

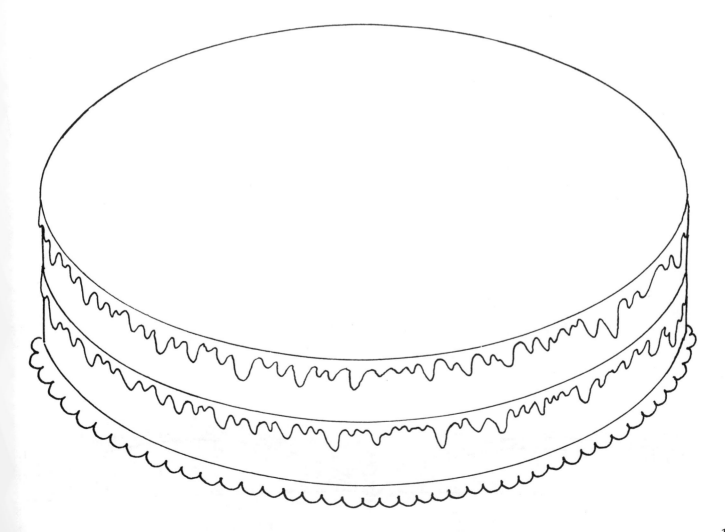

What do you think the *Book of Life* might look like?

Show what it might have been like to have been Jonah inside of the whale.

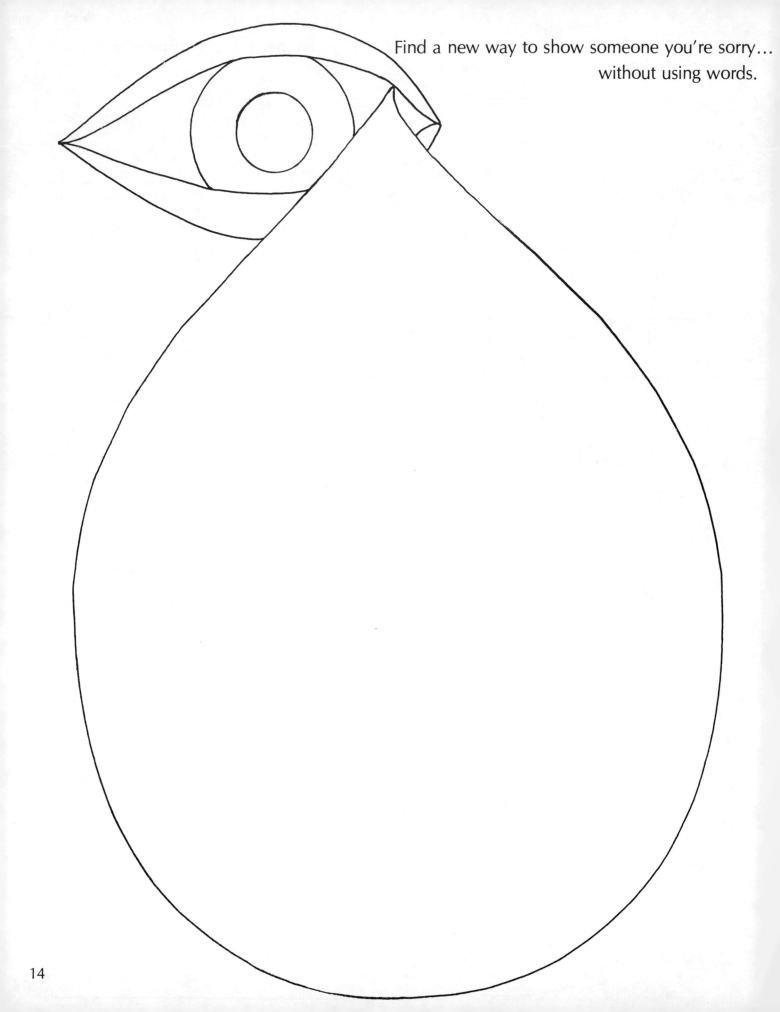

Find a new way to show someone you're sorry...
without using words.

14

Guess what you would have seen at a Yom Kippur celebration 1000 years ago. Guess what you might see at a Yom Kippur celebration 1000 years from now.

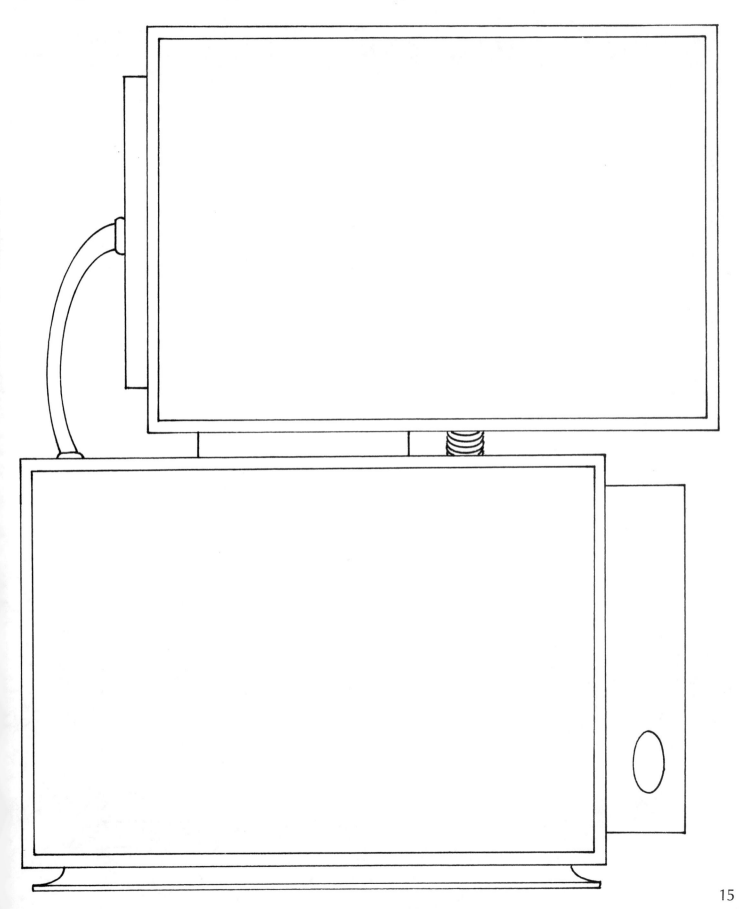

Imagine lying on your back and gazing up through the roof of your Sukkah...at midnight.

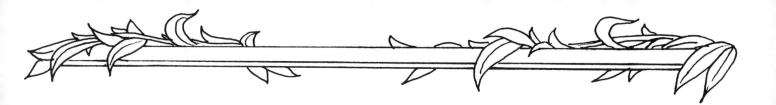

Build a unique Sukkah and decorate it with some really unusual things.

Design an original, one-of-a-kind, Simchat Torah flag.

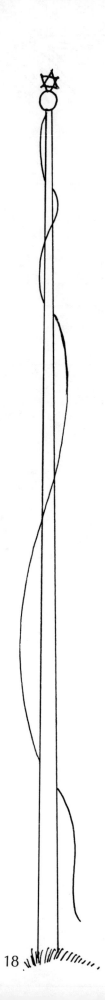

On Simchat Torah we begin reading the story of how God created the world in seven days. What would you have wanted God to create if there had been an 8th day of creation?

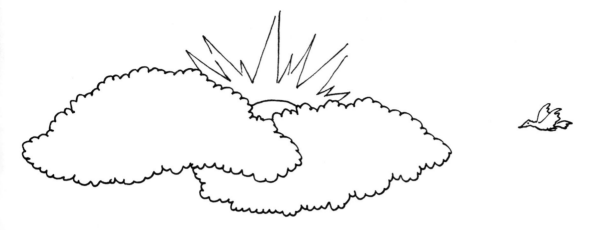

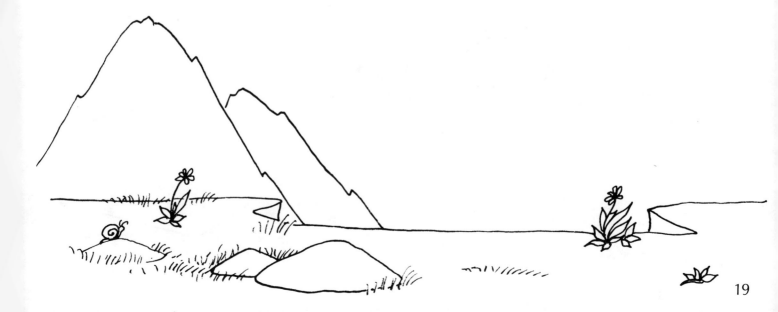

Show the silliest Hanukkah gift in the world.

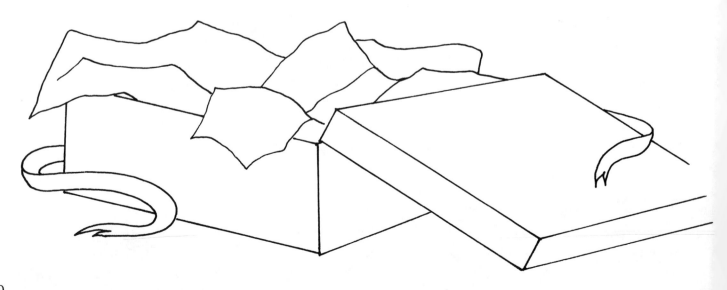

Guess what a Hanukkah menorah will look like in the year 2500.

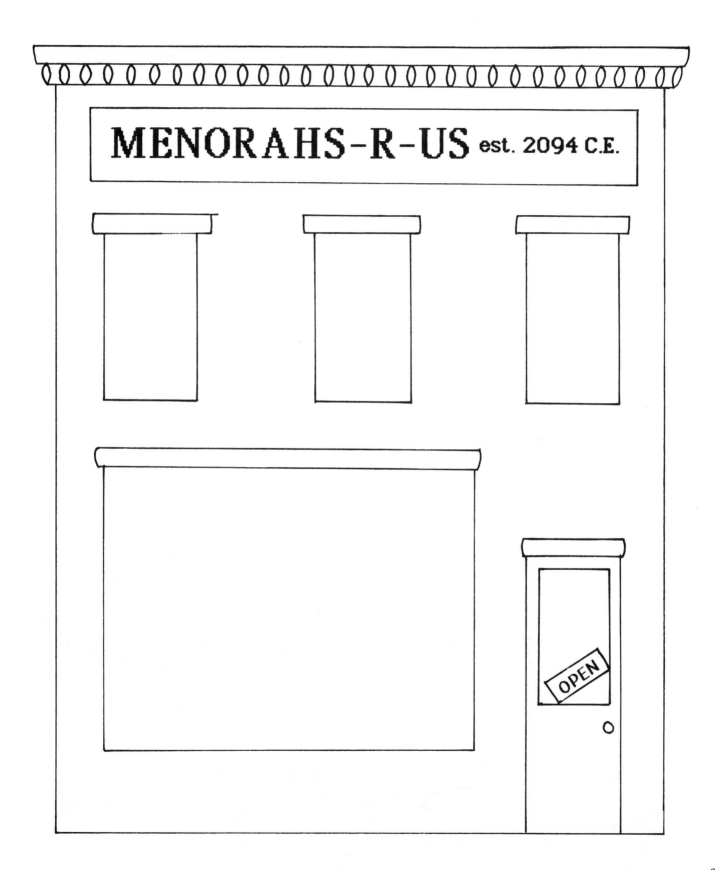

MENORAHS-R-US est. 2094 C.E.

OPEN

Make up a new game to play with a dreidel.

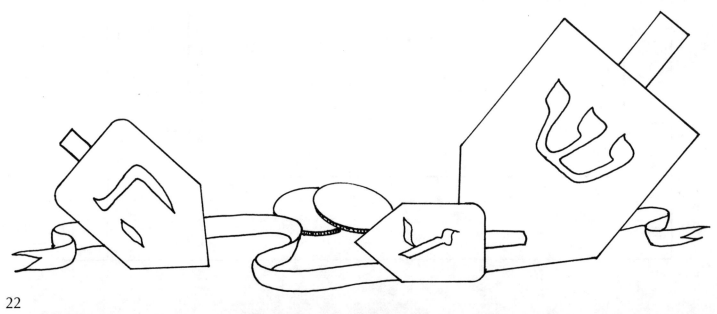

Pretend that you were a Maccabee. Draw your most exciting part in the Hanukkah story.

Create a video game for Hanukkah.

What do you think about as you watch the Hanukkah candles burning?

"Grow" a tree that produces something unlike anything produced by a tree before.

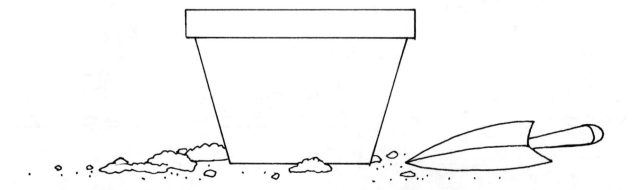

Design a new invention for taking care of trees.
Show how it works.

Draw your family tree.

Design a Be-Kind-To-Trees bumper sticker.

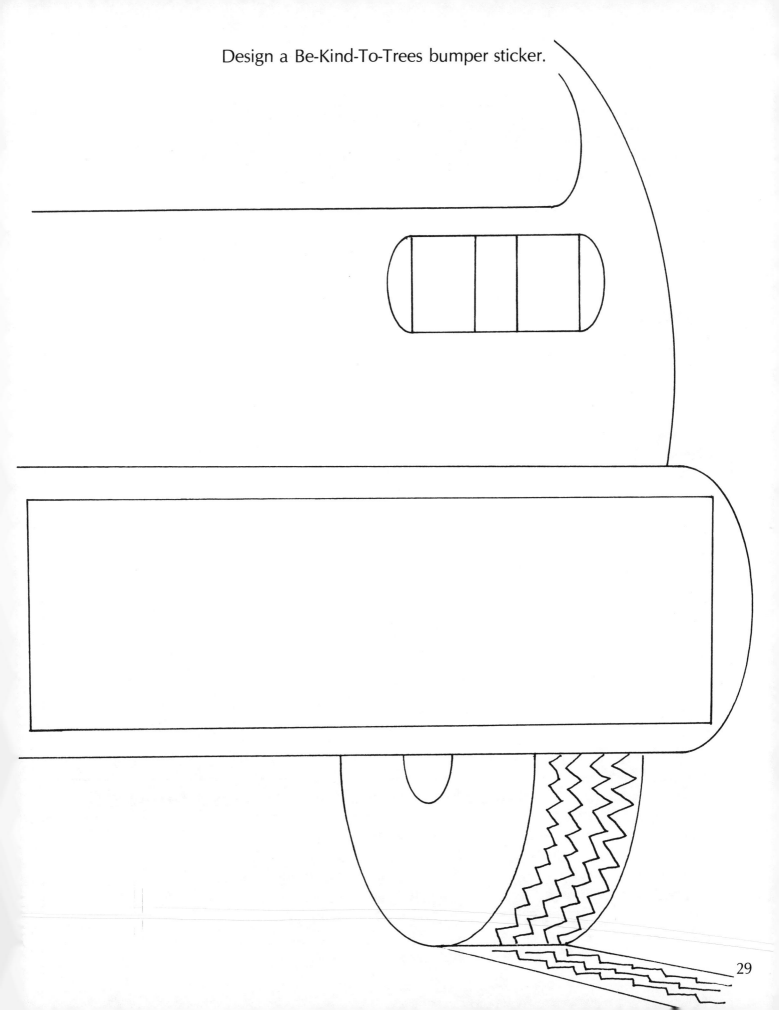

If Mordechai saved your life, how would you reward him?

Picture yourself wearing the most outrageous costume in the Purim parade.

MOST OUTRAGEOUS !

Imagine something really surprising inside your Shalach Manot package.

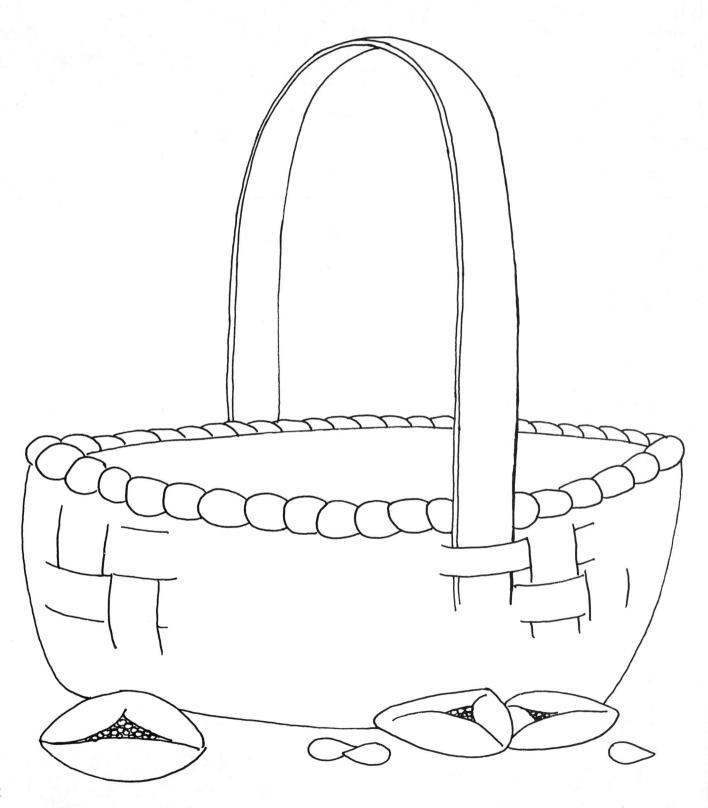

What's an unusual use for a grogger on the day *after* Purim?

Draw the most superfantabulous hiding place for an afikomen.

Can you imagine what the slaves in Egypt might have daydreamed about?

35

Suppose that Moses touched the Red Sea with his rod and, instead of parting, the water did something even stranger.

What would you have packed for your 40-year walk through the desert?

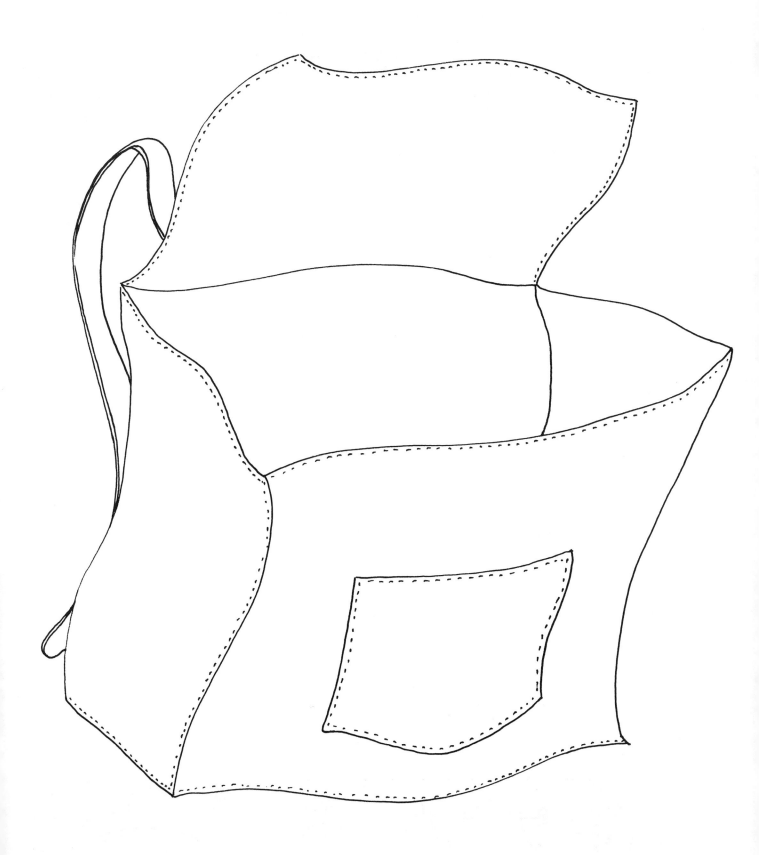

If you could invite anyone to your seder, who would it be?

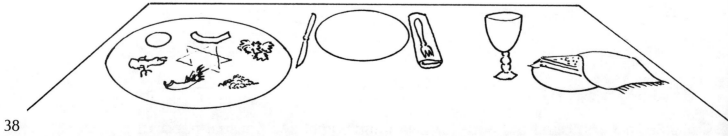

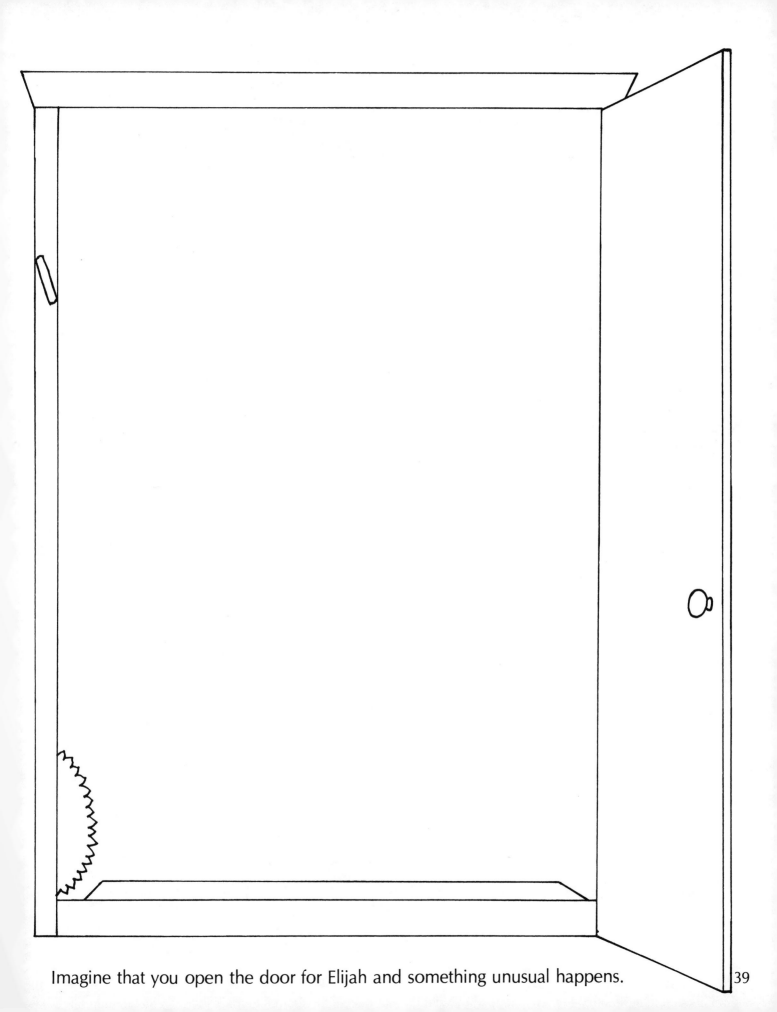

Imagine that you open the door for Elijah and something unusual happens.

Design a special Yom Ha'atzmaut T-shirt.

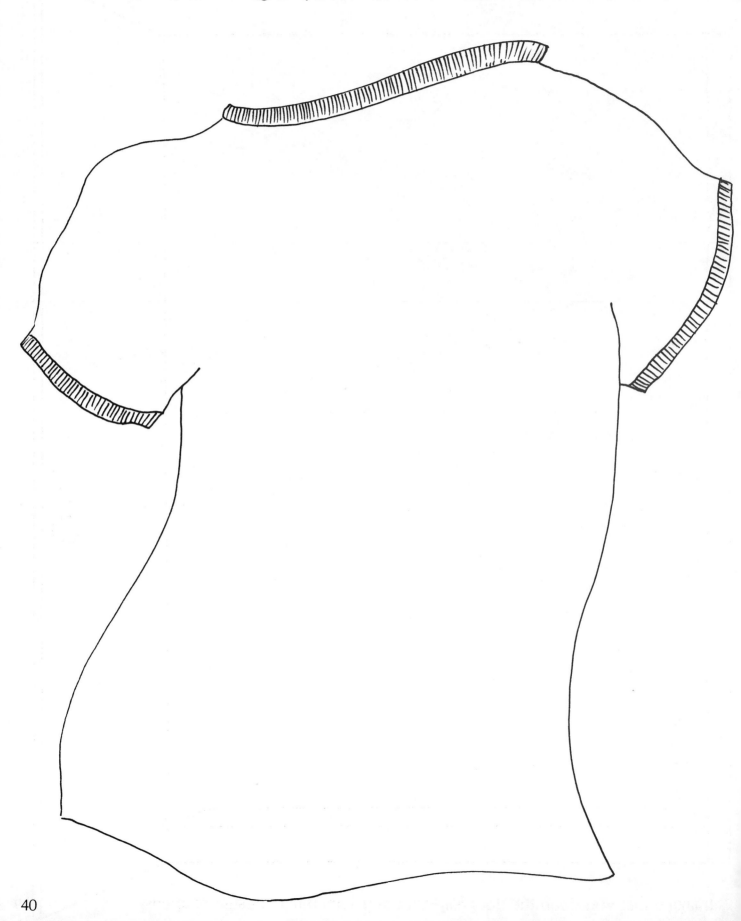

Some fireworks make pictures when they explode.
Design a Yom Ha'atzmaut fireworks display.

Draw a map like one young scholars might have followed to Shimon bar Yohai's cave. Remember you want to confuse the Romans.

Turn this cave into a modern-day classroom.

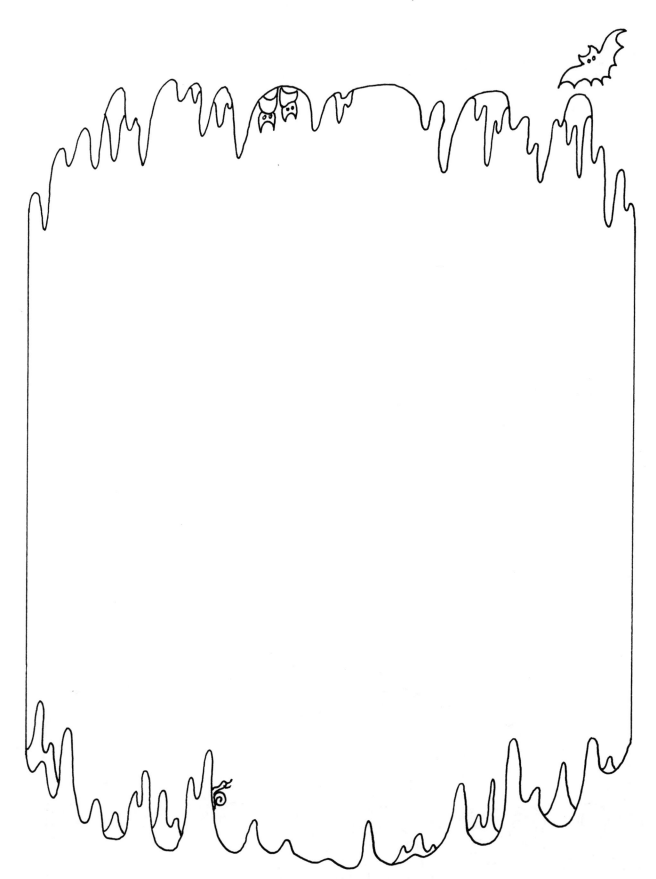

It is said that we were all present at the giving of the Ten Commandments at Mount Sinai. Draw yourself there.

44

On Shavuot, some people place a crown of flowers on the Torah. Others place a crown of flowers on their own heads. Design a crown of flowers for Shavuot.

Tips for Encouraging Artistic Expression

1. Foster imagination and new directions of thought. It is important to refrain from imposing adult standards and ideas on children, from interfering with too many questions, and from encouraging great similarity among the products of different children.

2. Allow for experimentation with many different age-appropriate drawing materials:

   Ages 5-8: crayons (assorted sizes and colors), colored-chalk, felt-tip pens, pencils (regular and colored), ball-point pens

   Ages 8-10: same as above plus charcoal, oil pastels, colored markers

   Be sure to provide work space and plenty of TIME, too.

3. Provide a wide variety of topic-related background experiences, such as holiday stories, films, tapes, songs, speakers, or model ceremonies.

4. Be an enthusiatic role model by showing an interest in both the holiday topic and the art process.

5. Encourage the children to discuss and evaluate their own work. Exhibit the work non-judgmentally.

6. Review your own art background. Feel free to expand upon it and to share what you have learned with your children.

Don't Stop There!
Creative Ways to Expand Upon Drawing Adventures

It's easy to expand upon the drawing adventures in this book! Here are some ideas to help you get started:

Substitute Other Projects for Drawing Activities

Substituting another project for a drawing activity can be as simple as constructing a picture with felt pieces instead of with crayons. Here is a partial list of other projects that can be done by following the directions on an activity page and then using interesting materials to complete the assignment:

banners, batiks, bulletin boards, bumper stickers, buttons, cartoons, ceramics, collages, comics, designs, diagrams, etchings, films, flannel boards, graphics, illustrations, lithographs, macrame, masks, mobiles, montages, murals, needlework, origami, paintings, papier mache, patterns, pennants, photos, postcards, posters, prints, puppets, quilts, scrapbooks, sculptures, shadow boxes, silk screen, stained "glass" (plastic), string art, tie-dye, triptychs, wall hangings, weavings, and woodwork.

Elaborate Upon Drawing Activities

After completing a drawing activity, use the illustration as a blueprint or basis for other projects. Perhaps the drawing can be the inspiration for a poem or skit. Examples of elaboration might also include:

advertisements, announcements, articles, audio tapes, ballads, billboards, books, collections, costumes, dances, debates, demonstrations, discussions, displays, drama, editorials, essays, exhibits, flags, games, graffiti, greeting cards, interviews, jingles, jokes, journals, kits, learning centers, letters, lists, models, music, myths, newscasts, oral reports, outlines, pamphlets, parties, quizzes, radio programs, recipes, reenactments, rhymes, simulations, slogans, stories, surveys, tape recordings, transparencies, want ads, and warnings.

About the Author and the Artist

Marji Gold-Vukson was born in Stamford, Connecticut and, by the time she was a senior in high school, had lived in 7 different cities, 12 different houses, and had attended 11 different schools. In more recent years, Marji settled long enough to receive her Masters of Science in Education from Purdue University, to teach elementary public and religious school classes, and to collaborate with her husband, Micheal, on four kids and ten books.

Micheal Gold-Vukson grew up in Mendota and DePue, Illinois. He is currently completing work on his Ph.D. in Art Education from Purdue University, teaching elementary art classes on the faculty of the Lafayette Indiana School Corporation, and, along with his wife, Marji, is raising four artistically-creative little Gold-Vuksons.